1776

THE INFINITY ENGINES: MISSIONS

ANDREW HASTIE

Published by Here Be Dragons Ltd.

ISBN: 978-1-9164747-2-7

5.6

1

PRESIDENT'S DAY

[FBI Headquarters, New York. Date: Monday, January 17, 2018]

Working over the President's Day weekend was the worst.

Special Agent John Anderson slouched behind his desk watching thousands of lines of code compile. His work on image processing was part of a major upgrade that was going to take over six months to roll out. It was ahead of schedule — which was how he knew he'd seriously annoyed his boss. The chance to get home for the weekend and spend a few days with his mother disappeared in the time it took to open the roster email.

Everyone else in his section would be carving turkeys and cracking open beers, while he sat staring at lines of code and running recognition tests.

His latest improvements were pretty awesome. Most AIs could distinguish a car from a truck, a person from a tree, but the functionality he was working on could recognize erratic behavior, subtle changes in an individual's body language. His code was going to help identify the 'Lone Wolf' — the terrorist working alone and help stop him before he drove his minivan into a crowd of people or shot up a school.

It was a quarter-to-five and his floor was unusually quiet. A tech team was busy installing a new server into the line of dark grey cabinets along the back wall. Each one of the units cost more than the average American made in a lifetime. Their processing power enhanced by GPUs that were originally developed for bitcoin mining. *Bet they're on double-time,* Anderson thought, *unless they've also said something dumb in front of their boss.*

It was his first year as a specialist in the analysis section, supporting the operational branches of the Counter Terrorism Division of the FBI. Their daily meeting was usually a stand-up, a ten-minute briefing where no one got to sit down, which was meant to keep it short and focused. Assistant Director Masterson was head of the Communications Exploitation Section. She'd worked on Operation Ghost Click and had taken down numerous botnets — which made her something of a legend within the electronic crime community and was also a highly respected member of the National Cyber Investigative Joint Task Force. To top it all she had a double-first from Harvard in applied mathematics.

All good reasons why he shouldn't have corrected her.

He blamed his father. The old man was a stickler for facts. As a history professor at Yale, he may not have been the best role model for diplomacy, but his dad had always taught him to state the facts, not to embellish, just say it straight.

So, when Masterson had made some joke about the President's birthday, Anderson couldn't help himself.

President Franklin was born on 17th January 1706.

Except he wasn't.

As his father had taken great pleasure in explaining at every holiday meal for the last twenty years. 'The Gregorian calendar didn't come in to common use in the United States for another forty-six years.'

As he carved the steaming turkey onto white china plates, he would remind them: 'The colonies were still using the Julian calendar. Franklin would have been born on January 6th 1705, courtesy of Augustus Caesar's refinements in 8BC.'

Anderson had heard the story so many times it had embedded itself, like a muscle memory. Looking back, he realized that the repetition could have been early signs of his father's impending dementia.

When Masterson brought up the holiday at the end of their meeting, the words of his father's anecdote came straight out of his mouth.

The Assistant Director had a well-practiced array of expressions intended to freeze your blood. Her glare could burn into your soul until there was nothing left but a smoking hole and the way her lip twisted as he interrupted her reminded him of a wolf preparing to rip your throat out.

'Since you seem to know so much about this particular holiday,' she snarled. 'I'll take that into account when I'm preparing the roster.'

The others had looked at him with pity; he was the most junior member of the team and still a rookie, it was a stupid mistake and he'd paid the price. They'd all got to go home for the weekend.

Sipping his coffee, he watched the technicians wheel in another matte-black server and slide it carefully into the rack. The Guardian system was the most powerful surveillance platform on the planet. Anderson had no idea how much it actually cost to run, but the CTD budget was $8 billion and he was pretty sure most of it went into the real-time detection systems that were displayed across the large wall of screens at the far end of the office.

Behind the graphs and constantly updating data feeds were millions of CPUs processing billions of data points instantaneously. Machine learning and AI algorithms were grinding through petabytes of information looking for patterns, searching for any suspicious activity.

Beyond the constant cyber threats from Russia, China and the organized syndicates of botnets from the eastern bloc, there was the analysis of millions of CCTV video streams, social media and cell phone activity.

It had been a quiet weekend. No high-level threats had been detected and there was nothing much left to do but commit his code back and log off. He checked his cell phone. There were two messages, one from Mel Baker and the other from Steve Jones; both were picture messages showing how much fun they were having on their day off, but there was nothing from his mom — she would be at the care home by now, trying to feed his dad with a plastic spoon.

Anderson was putting on his jacket as a suspicious activity alert flashed up on one of his screens. He tapped on the icon and a window expanded to show a video feed from one of the national monuments.

It was Mount Vernon, the memorial to General Washington, and there was a crazy guy dressed in the unmistakable red coat of a British soldier from the War of Independence, stepping over the rope towards one of the exhibits.

The Guardian report showed that the Fairfax Police were already responding, so he killed the alert and turned off his monitor.

It was 16:55 and no one was expecting him to hang around. They would be serving mojitos down at the Delancey, and one of his favorite bands would be warming up. If he left now he could be in the roof garden bar in twenty minutes.

2

HOME

[Greenwich Village, New York. Date: Tuesday, January 18, 2018]

Anderson's phone went off at 06:00. Not with the usual dulcet tones of his alarm, but with an angry buzzing, like a bee trapped in a box.

Someone was trying to break through the do-not-disturb rules by ringing twice in three minutes.

The room was dark, and he had no idea where the phone was. His hangover held him down against the bed like a pro wrestler and when he tried to open his eyes there was a horrible moment of nausea, so he shut them and surrendered his head to the pillow.

The buzzing stopped and a couple of seconds later was replaced by a series of pings — messages.

Anderson had no idea what time he'd gone to bed. He remembered getting to the Delancey, the band and the first couple of rounds, but he must have got really drunk — the kind of drunk that obliterates all traces of memory. When he finally made it back to his apartment, he found that all her stuff was gone. Isobel had walked out on New Year's Day, over two weeks ago, but she'd waited until the holiday weekend to collect her things.

There wasn't a trace of her left, as though she'd just been erased from his life, but he guessed that's what you got when you hooked up with a forensic scientist.

They'd met in week six of training at the academy in Quantico, both new recruits and both trying to cram for the theory test the next day.

It was late in the evening on a Sunday and the library had been virtually empty. He wasn't a fan of books, or reading, and had only come in to use the computers. Isobel was the opposite, she had her pretty little nose buried in a book and was completely unaware of him — or so he'd thought.

The tests were all computerized, and Anderson had logged onto the system to practice, it had taken less than twenty minutes to realize he was going to fail badly.

He groaned loudly, and Isobel looked up.

She held the book up. 'You're not going to do the theory?'

Anderson shrugged. 'Not much of a reader.'

There was a glint in her eye. A precision about the way she put the manual down that should have warned him, but he was drawn to her — she was like a cat toying with a mouse. 'My mom says books are the closest thing to magic.'

He laughed, 'she should meet my father, they'd get along famously.'

'Is he a librarian too?'

Anderson shook his head. 'History Professor, at Yale.'

She seemed impressed. 'Is he married?'

'To the college, yeah. Mom left a while back, but I don't think he's on the market.'

'Shame,' she purred, touching her ear nonchalantly. 'My mother likes clever men.'

'And what about you?'

'Oh, apparently I have terrible taste. She's hated every one of my boyfriends — says I always go for the dysfunctional ones.'

He laughed. 'You're a fixer.'

'What's that?'

'Someone who believes they can solve the world's problems.'

She smiled. 'And what are you?'

'A failure,' he said, pointing to the screen. 'Don't suppose you want to help me?'

And so it began.

After Quantico, they'd been assigned to different field offices and for months they'd worked apart, seeing each other at weekends. The absence extended the honeymoon period and made for some very wild and crazy reunions.

For a while it helped with nightmares, balancing the new job and the insatiable girlfriend had exhausted him to the point where he would collapse into a dreamless sleep.

Then they moved into the apartment and things began to change.

Before Anderson met her, he used to drink himself to sleep or work through the night and wake up with his face pressed into the keyboard. Anything to avoid staring at the bedroom ceiling for hours.

Once their passion had levelled out and daily routines

were firmly established, the insomnia returned, and he found himself lying next to her every night trying to fall asleep. She hadn't noticed at first, but then it got so bad that he began to make excuses about coming to bed.

When she insisted that he see a doctor he was forced to tell her the truth. This wasn't a new thing, he'd tried all the drugs: Trazodone, Halcion and a whole range of anti-depressants — none of them worked.

The nightmares still came.

He dreamed he was drowning, waking up in a cold sweat, unable to catch his breath. They thought it was some kind of sleep apnea, but the tests said otherwise.

Their relationship was based on a lie and it took her less than two years to uncover the damage that he'd hidden so carefully from everyone else.

She would have been an asset to the profiling division if she ever got bored with scenes-of-crime. He told her that on the day she left, shouted it down the hall as she gathered her bags and went through the door.

She didn't look back, her shoulders hunched against the rain as she went down the front steps and he knew then that he was never going to see her again.

3

SECOND SIGHTING

Masterson looked angry, even more angry than usual. She'd been called on Monday night after the intrusion at Mount Vernon had developed in a rather unexpected way. One that Anderson should have picked up on, if he hadn't been so keen to get to the bar.

It turned out that the crazy homeless guy, who Anderson assumed was trying to get himself locked up for the night, was actually a magician. Masterson was in the middle of explaining this to the rest of the team in the briefing room when he crept in and took a seat at the back.

'This is the footage from the Washington memorial at Mount Vernon,' she said, pointing to the large screen. It showed the old man in his red coat stepping over the barrier. 'As you can see from the timestamp it was 16:55 when he tried to steal the exhibit.'

'Guardian picked this up six minutes later.' A second window opened to show a video of what looked like the same guy trying to break into one of the cabinets in the Smithsonian at 17:01.

Just after I left, thought Anderson.

Once he found his phone, he discovered that it had been inundated with messages. *Probably shouldn't have ignored it* — he thought, but he'd assumed it had been Isobel.

'They can't be the same guy,' said one of the team. 'There's no way he could get there in six minutes.'

Masterson raised one eyebrow and nodded to Joe Davies, who smiled as he stood up to take over the briefing. He was her current golden boy, but it wouldn't last — everyone knew what a hard-ass bitch she was to work for.

Davies opened up the Guardian system and they watched as it processed the video feeds from both sites. The data points multiplied as the algorithms that Anderson had helped to develop compared every possible angle of his face, analyzed the gait of his walk, even measuring the distance between his strides, until it confirmed that it was the same person. An e-Pic of a man in his late fifties with a bushy red beard appeared on one side of the screen with the words 'Subject Unknown,' beneath them.

The Guardian was hooked into the Interstate Photo System. As part of the war on terror it had been developed to access identity records on virtually every adult who'd ever been in the USA.

'He's not in the database,' Davies declared, ignoring the fact that he was in two different locations that were at least thirty minutes' drive away from each other.

'But how did he get across town so fast?' asked Baker.

Anderson liked Baker, she was a woman who just said it the way it was.

Masterson spoke up. 'We don't know, but we have him in custody. He resisted arrest and one of the guards had to taser him. He should be ready to interview in the next couple of hours.'

The video feed switched to a shot of a police cell. The old man was stretched out on a bed as if he were asleep.

'What was he after?' asked Baker.

'No idea. Davies you lead on this and Baker can assist. Anderson see me in my office.'

4

ADMINISTRATIVE DUTIES

Masterson's office was a shrine to order and tidiness. Hanging on the walls were the various accolades she'd achieved in her ten years of service, including the FBI Medal for Meritorious Achievement, which she'd had framed with a photograph of her and the Director of the Bureau.

'Do we have a problem?' she asked, without looking up from her computer.

'No Ma'am.'

'You left the office at 1700 hours precisely.'

'It was the end of my shift.'

She looked up over the rims of her designer glasses, the tone of her voice growing stern. 'You didn't think to investigate the incident in Fairfax?'

'The local PD had it under control. I didn't think it constituted a risk to national security.'

Masterson's eyes narrowed. 'I don't get you Anderson. You're a talented analyst and a first-class developer, but your work ethic is career-limiting to say the least.'

Anderson wasn't about to go into the fact that his love

life was a car crash, or that his sleep patterns were totally out of whack. So he used his dad.

'My father's been admitted to Mount Sinai.'

It wasn't entirely untrue. His dad had gone into dementia care over six months ago. His mother had moved back to help with the transition, although she may as well have stayed in Florida since his father had no idea who she was.

Masterson's expression softened slightly, as he knew it would. 'Do you need to take some personal time?'

'No ma'am, work keeps me focused.'

She made a note on his record. 'I'm taking you off the project and putting you on administrative duties. Just until your head's back in the game.'

Administrative duties meant that Anderson got to spend the rest of the morning writing up executive summaries of status reports. Amongst the usual script-kiddies and DDoS attacks were several serious attempts to take down the power grid. He was happy to read that the US defenses had repelled them. The report showed they originated from somewhere deep within China, using hacked switches in the Ukraine to route all their traffic and mask their tracks. There was no way to know exactly where, since once any trace hit the Chinese network it went dark. Nothing got past their perimeter defenses, they called it the Great Firewall of China, and just like its namesake, it was one seriously solid piece of engineering.

An email notification appeared in the corner of his screen. It was from Baker, and the subject read: 'Time traveler?'

He opened the email to find there was nothing but a

shortened URL. Anderson recognized the provider, it was one of those links that expired after you opened it — a burner.

He opened a tor browser and pasted the link into it. Their computer usage was continually logged but since his job was to trawl the dark web it was not unusual for him to anonymize himself — most of the tools they used were invented inside the American military anyway.

The site was a collection of images, a pinterest board of numerous pictures of the same guy — 'Dark Santa' as some of the team had started to call him. Baker had run a standard search on the old man, her systems crawled the web and other digital archives using face recognition.

Many of the photographs were old, some looked like they had been taken from documents going back to the early 1840s. There he was, the same mad pair of eyes staring out from scenes that spanned the last two hundred years.

It made no sense, Anderson thought, there was no way the same man could have been there at the Siege of Vicksburg and fifty years later be standing behind President Woodrow Wilson at his inauguration.

He closed the browser and looked over at Baker. She shrugged, it was a subtle gesture for her. One of them was going to have to go and show it to Masterson and he could tell from her expression that it wasn't going to be her.

His desk phone rang. It was the Assistant Director.

'Anderson.'

'Ma'am'

'I want you to drive over to Fairfax with Davies and check the discrepancies in the time coding on their systems.'

Anderson was about to protest that he was an intelligence analyst not a field agent, but anything was better than writing reports.

'Yes Ma'am.'

He put the phone down and unlocked his desk drawer, taking out the Glock 22. It was something he'd only ever used on a firing range, but it was standard procedure to carry it when he was out in the field.

5

MOUNT VERNON

[Mount Vernon, Fairfax County, Virginia]

They'd driven for four hours in virtual silence. Davies wasn't interested in small talk. The day after the holiday meant the I-95 was quieter than usual, most people added personal days onto the long weekend to extend the break. Anderson had to remind himself that this was supposed to be his day off too, but he didn't care that much — there was no one to enjoy it with, and so he closed his eyes, letting his hangover take over.

Mount Vernon was a beautiful white clapperboard house, on the Potomac river. The home of Martha Washington, who had dedicated it to the memory of her husband, the Commander of the Continental army, and the hero who'd died fighting for American independence.

Anderson knew the museum well. His father had brought him to the site every year, like some kind of pilgrimage. There was a real sense of history about the place.

Somehow being around Washington's memorabilia made it come to life.

The security detail waved them through at the gates, they'd been warned in advance, but the government plates on their car would have given them access anyhow. Isobel used to hate it when he would take a pool car out for the weekend just to get free parking.

They were shown into the monitoring suite by the head of security, a stiff-necked ex-marine called Wilson, who was looking a little anxious. There would be difficult questions to answer, like how he let a man dressed as a two hundred-year-old British soldier onto the grounds, let alone into the collection.

The footage of the incident was already loaded up on the screens. Nine different views of the same event played out on a loop. Each shot showing the same red-coated man trying to break open the case.

'What's in the display?' asked Davies.

Wilson folded his arms. 'Washington's dentures.'

'His teeth.'

Wilson nodded.

Before Davies could ask why, Anderson cut in. 'Do your systems synchronize with the public time servers?'

He could see that Wilson hadn't got a clue, this wasn't a question he was expecting. His eyes flicked away and up, interrogation training had taught Anderson that this was a usual sign of someone searching deep memories for an answer.

'I guess, but I don't see the relevance.'

No, thought Anderson, *you're waiting for us to ask how he got away*.

'They're connected to the national time servers,' advised the operator.

Anderson checked his watch, the times on the screens matched exactly.

Davies looked impatiently at Anderson, like he was somehow his superior — which he wasn't. 'So, where did he go?'

'No idea,' shrugged Wilson. 'The cameras blacked out for about twenty seconds. All we got was static.'

The operator released the loop and they watched as the screens went dark for eighteen seconds and then flickered back to life.

'Did he take anything?'

'Not as far as we can tell.'

6

INTERVIEW

[Washington Police Department, Washington DC]

The old guy sat in the chair on the other side of the table. He was a big man, easily over six-foot tall and at least two-hundred-and-sixty pounds. Like a bear in an overcoat he struggled to stay still, constantly adjusting his seat, or scratching his beard. The handcuffs looked like a child's toy around his wrist and Anderson thought he could probably snap them just as easily if he wanted to.

But he hadn't, the guy had been well behaved since he'd been arrested. The report was light on personal details, in fact there was no background at all, except for his name: Colonel Rufius Westinghouse. Which Anderson had guessed was an honorific he'd taken to go with the uniform.

After they left Mount Vernon, Davies had driven them up to the Smithsonian along the Potomac river, moaning about how this case was going to end up making him late for the Knicks game. Anderson just stared out the window at the view. The time hadn't been wrong on the Mount Vernon system, he wondered what would happen if it turned out to be correct at the museum too.

They got a similar story from the Smithsonian security team. The colonel simply turned up, somehow avoiding the guards at the main entrance and headed straight for one of the Washington exhibits. Fortunately, one of their officers was able to take him down before he could do any damage. There was nothing wrong with the timing on their system either.

The Metropolitan P.D. had thrown him in the drunk tank. The sergeant searched him when he came in, still comatose from the taser and found nothing but a weird antique watch and an old book full of blank pages.

They were sitting in evidence bags on the table between them.

Davies was taking the lead on the interview, which suited Anderson. He pretended to take notes so he could study the old hobo, observe his reactions to the questions.

'Your full name is Colonel Rufius Westinghouse?' Davies began, flicking through the arrest report.

The man nodded, his eyes fixed on Anderson.

'For the purpose of the tape please answer yes or no.'

'Rufius Vainglorious Westinghouse,' he said in a broad British accent.

That's why he's not in the database, noted Anderson.

'Can you give me an address?'

Westinghouse shook his head.

'No fixed abode,' Davies said aloud, writing onto the form.

'Do you understand why you were detained?'

The old man shrugged, his eyes lost their focus and glazed over a little.

'Can you tell me what year this is?' Anderson asked when there was no response.

The colonel counted on his fingers for a few seconds. 'Twelve thousand and eighteen?'

Davies frowned and put the file down. 'Do you know who the President is?'

Anderson knew these were standard questions that the bureau used to assess confusion, to determine the lucidity of an individual.

The old man leaned forward and grinned at Davies. 'Do you?'

'Please answer the question sir.'

The colonel turned and addressed Anderson directly. 'Do you have a dollar bill?'

Anderson nodded.

'May I see it?'

He pulled one out and held it up, so the old man could look at it.

'Franklin?' He grimaced. 'It's worse than I thought.'

'President Franklin was the founder of our country.'

'Benjamin Franklin was indeed one of the founders, but he was a better Secretary of State,' he said, standing up and rattling his handcuffs. 'I need to go.'

That's what my father used to say about Franklin, thought Anderson.

Davies glanced at Anderson, his eyes widening a little.

He thinks he's crazy.

'Where are you going sir?' asked Anderson.

The old man scratched his beard. 'Seventy-six most likely. Assuming I can find the right artefact.'

Davies opened the file once more and took out his pen. 'Seventy-six, is that an address?'

'Of sorts, although most people would call it a year.'

'Like nineteen seventy-six?' asked Anderson.

The colonel pulled nonchalantly on the chain that connected him to the chair. 'Try seventeen seventy-six.'

'And why that particular year?' asked Anderson.

'I need to prevent the assassination of George Washington.'

Davies was packing his stuff into the trunk of the Chevrolet Suburban when Anderson walked out of the station.

'He's just another crazy off his meds,' he said, slamming the door on the SUV. 'This was a total waste of time. You want a ride back to the station?'

Anderson shook his head. 'I need to go back over the footage at the Smithsonian. Still don't have a clear explanation for the time discrepancy.'

Davies shrugged and opened the driver's door. 'Suit yourself. See you tomorrow.'

Anderson watched Davies pull out onto Indiana Avenue and turned back towards the Police headquarters.

He had a few more questions for the crazy old man.

7

FALSE TEETH

'Forgotten something?' asked the colonel, when Anderson returned to the interview room.

He took out his phone and placed it on the table. 'Just a few more questions. Do you mind if I record this?' he asked, opening the memo app.

The colonel laughed. 'You can try. I tend to have an adverse effect on technology.' He cleared his throat and took a long drink of water as if getting ready for the interview.

'I wanted to ask you about the artefacts you were trying to steal. The first was George Washington's dentures.'

The colonel bared his teeth and tapped them together. 'The General didn't have the best set of gnashers. They say he was down to a single tooth by the time he died.'

'Can you tell me what you were going to do with them?'

'So, you're going to think this sounds a little odd,' the old man began, leaning forward and placing his hands on the table, 'but the secret to navigating the past is all in the quality of the artefact you choose. Man-made objects are the best, preferably ones that have had direct contact with the subject — and let's face it you can't get much better than a pair of false teeth, can you?'

'You can't get much better, no,' Anderson agreed, using a negotiation technique called "mirroring", where you repeated key words from their last sentence. It was supposed to put the subject at ease and get them to trust you.

This old man had invented a whole new kind of crazy, and it was fascinating.

Anderson took out a pen and made some notes. 'So, once you had the dentures you could travel back to 1776? How would you do that exactly? Do you have a time machine?'

'What, like a DeLorean?' the colonel sniggered. 'This isn't like a movie you know. It's not something just anyone can do. The past is a wilderness and the timeline of an artefact is like a map, a trail that makes it easier for us to locate the right moment. Otherwise you could end up God knows where.'

'Us? There are more of you?'

'There's an entire Order.' He nodded. 'Not that you'd know it up here at the frontier. Most of them stay out of the twenty-first, too much interference — especially for the Copernicans. They like the sixteenth, nothing like a pre-Industrial period to keep the clackers happy.'

There was a knock at the door, the red-faced sergeant was staring at Anderson through the glass and holding up five fingers.

'Time for one last question,' said the colonel.

'Why do you want to save General Washington?'

The colonel's expression changed as he thought about his answer. Anderson wasn't sure if he'd crossed some kind of line with the question. Isobel had read a study on the motivation of psychopaths and how the last thing you should ever do is ask them to explain their actions.

'Have you ever wished you could go back and change something?' he asked. 'Something in your past that you knew would make your life better?'

I would save my sister, Anderson thought, *stop her from taking that bend.*

'We all have something,' the old man continued, reading the pain in Anderson's silence. 'Now imagine what it would be like to know you could do that on a wider historical scale. To see the benefit of saving one man and the effect it could have on a nation.'

'But the consequences?'

'Have been assessed.'

Anderson stopped the recording and put his phone away, reminding himself that this was supposed to be a technical investigation not some bat-shit crazy x-file.

'So, how exactly did you get from Mount Vernon in Fairfax to the Smithsonian in less than ten minutes?'

The colonel pointed at the watch in the evidence bag. 'The tachyon.'

'The watch?'

'Does a lot more than just tell the time. It's a Mark V, it has a torch.'

'And you can use it to teleport?'

'I don't think you're taking me seriously,' growled the old man.

'Sorry,' Anderson apologized, picking up the evidence bag, 'but you're telling me you can use this to move eighteen miles in under ten minutes.'

'Would have been quicker, but I think the damn thing's on the blink.'

'Of course,' Anderson said, as the sergeant reappeared. 'Thank you for your cooperation.'

'Is that it?'

Anderson got to his feet and picked up the other evidence bag. 'For now. The local police will take care of you and assign a legal representative.'

He walked over to the door and tapped on the glass.

'Pulvis et umbra sumus,' said the colonel with a wave.

8

DUST AND SHADOW

The phrase bugged Anderson all the way back on the train.

'Pulvis et umbra sumus.'

It was from Horace, he knew that because it was one of his father's favorite quotes.

'We are but dust and shadow.'

Anderson didn't believe in coincidences, everything happened for a reason, but there was no way the crazy old fool could have known that it was how his father used to say goodbye.

It was dark by the time he got back to Greenwich Village. The heating in his apartment was broken and the place was colder than the inside of his fridge, which was also empty. Without Isobel, the place had lost its heart, it was just a box with some furniture, like a motel room, nothing more than a place to sleep.

Except he didn't sleep, not without a drink. The times when he closed his eyes and drifted off were long gone. She used to beg him to see a shrink, but that would have to go on his record, and the Bureau would start asking questions — not that they didn't know. Everyone was aware of what happened that night in Fairview.

It was late December and they were driving up to Wilsonville; his grandparents had a house on Lake Wallenpaupack and the whole family were supposed to be meeting there for Christmas. The roads were icy and there'd been an accident on the highway, so his sister took a back road.

Candice was ten years older than him, a bright, beautiful eighteen-year-old who'd just graduated from high school and spent the entire journey boring him rigid about what she was going to do at Yale.

Their parents were delayed at LAX waiting for the Newark runway to be cleared, and so she'd volunteered to take him, which was cool because she always let him sit in the front. Her car was an old Ford Orion, one that she'd bought with the money she'd made from her waitressing job — their father was a strong believer in learning the value of hard work.

The back road had been cleared by a snow plough that morning and he remembered thinking how shiny and black the road looked as it snaked through the white forest ahead of them.

At some point he'd fallen asleep, the car heaters were on full blast and he'd insisted on keeping his coat on. The temperature and the chilled beats of her music lulled him into a cozy dream.

The sound of his sister's scream woke him with a start.

The car hit the frozen lake and spiderweb cracks spread across the windscreen. Then water burst through. The white plane of sparkling ice disappeared as their car sank below the frozen surface. His sister was unconscious, blood was pouring down her face where she'd hit the steering wheel. Shouting her name, he struggled to release his seatbelt, but his fingers were numb from the cold and the water was filling up the car.

A local farmer saw the accident and found him floating face down on the surface.

Candice didn't make it.

The police report blamed black ice on the bend, coupled with worn treads on her tires. She'd lost traction on the corner and skidded straight into Fairview lake.

Anderson never went into water again, and every night he dreamed of drowning.

He couldn't stand the silence of the empty apartment, so he went down to Bobo's and ordered himself a drink and a steak sandwich.

The bar was warm and by the second beer he was beginning to thaw out. When the food came the waitress took away both empty bottles and left a third. Starting on the fries, he plugged his headphones into his phone and opened the recording he'd made of the interview.

It was mostly static.

There were snatches of conversation, but their voices were scrambled. Anderson knew there were devices that surveillance teams used to screw around with electronic listening, but there was no way that the old man would have known about that kind of technology.

He pulled the headphones out and opened his email.

There were six unread messages and he scanned the subject lines until he came to the one from Isobel. The line was like something from a break-up song.

'I know you won't want to hear this...'

He still hadn't opened it. He didn't need a 'Dear John' letter to know she wasn't coming back. His thumb swiped over it, revealing the delete option, but he still couldn't bring himself to do it.

Most of the other emails were just notifications he'd set up, automated reports and news digests of things he was interested in. The last one was from Baker. It read: 'Dark Santa has escaped!'

He opened the message. Apparently, the colonel had managed to over-power his guards on the way from the holding cell to the transport. Baker had even sent the CCTV footage of the incident, the old man knocked down his escort with one punch and ran into a closet, and never came back out.

It sent a shudder down Anderson's spine. This guy was starting to freak him out. He waved over the barman and ordered a bottle of Jack Daniel's. The evidence bags were still in his jacket pocket, he'd promised the sergeant that he would take them straight over to forensics, but for some reason he'd kept them.

He knew it was breaking protocol, but Anderson pulled the journal out of the ziplocked bag and examined it. The cover was leather, scratched and worn by time and use, but the pages were blank, the thick vellum-like paper untouched.

Who carries around an empty book? He asked himself, putting it to one side and taking out the watch.

The gold case was warm to the touch. It too was covered in scratches and nicks where it had been well-used. The thing was an antique, with a chain like an old pocket-watch, but the dial looked nothing like any clock he'd ever seen. It was made up of concentric rings, each one seemed to be rotating at a different speed.

There were two buttons on the side, like a stop watch. Anderson pressed the first one and the dials stopped and then started spinning back the opposite way.

Something happened to his drink.

The bottle was full, and his glass was empty.

He looked at the watch and the rings were moving clockwise again.

Anderson poured himself a very large drink.

9

SOMETHING'S CHANGED

[Wednesday, January 19, 2018]

Anderson woke up on the couch, still wearing his clothes and the remnants of a pizza in one hand with the rest scattered over the floor.

It was early, the drapes were open, and the sky was only just showing signs of dawn.

Someone was buzzing on his door.

'Okay,' he managed in a cracked, husky voice as he sat upright and waited for the world to straighten up.

There was a terrible taste in his mouth, he looked down at the half-eaten pizza and gagged, there were anchovies, Isobel hated anchovies.

The buzzer went again.

'Do you know what time it is?' he mumbled into the entry phone.

'It's Rufius Westinghouse, let me in.'

The colonel looked like a different man. He was wearing a

long greatcoat and a three-piece tweed suit. His hair was combed, and his beard trimmed, like something out of a Sherlock Holmes novel, or maybe he just got lucky in a thrift shop — Anderson was too hungover to care.

The old man took one look at the apartment and went to the kitchen to help himself to the coffee.

'You know I'm going to have to take you in,' Anderson said, searching the drawers for the Advil. He knocked back three of them with a glass of whisky.

The colonel handed him a steaming cup of coffee. 'I don't think you're in a fit state to take yourself in, let alone me.'

He picked up one of the evidence bags that was sitting on the kitchen worktop. 'Weren't you supposed to hand these over to forensics? Or did you find something you couldn't explain?'

Anderson suddenly remembered the watch. He'd got pretty messed up testing out that new drinking game.

'It takes you back two minutes.'

'One hundred and twenty-five seconds to be precise,' the colonel corrected him and pulled his journal out of the plastic bag. 'Did you read the almanac?'

Anderson shook his head. 'No, it was blank. But how does —'

'It's a tachyon mark V, the rewind function is only for emergencies. It appears that you may have some latent temporal abilities. I suspected as much when I first clapped eyes on you. You have that look — tell me, have you ever come close to dying?'

'What?'

'Near-death experiences can induce it. I've seen it happen a few times.' He put the watch back in his waistcoat and tucked the book inside his jacket.

'Hey, you can't take them, they're evidence.'

The colonel's eyes narrowed, and he folded his arms. 'Of what exactly?'

Anderson wished he could remember where he'd put his gun, something told him this guy wasn't going to come peacefully.

'You broke into two national institutions.'

'I walked in —'

'— and tried to steal a national treasure.'

'More like borrow it, actually. You wouldn't believe how many artefacts go missing every day. We tend to use them at night, so you don't notice.'

'Why?'

'As I explained before, it's the best way to get back to a specific event.' The colonel went over to the bookshelf and picked up the small wooden box that Anderson's father had given him for his eighth birthday. It contained an ammonite, a sixty-six million-year-old fossil. *History is not just in books,* his dad had written on the card inside.

'Printed material is especially useful as it tends to have a very stable timeline, but any man-made object will do.'

He held the wooden box in his hand and Anderson saw the air around it distort as fine ribbons of light wove out from it. He rubbed his eyes, but they were still there when he opened them again.

'We call it weaving. I can view the entire chronology of this artefact, where it's been, who's touched it. The day it was re-discovered in an old storeroom. Here,' He held out his hand, 'let me show you.'

Anderson spotted the Glock tucked down the side of the couch.

'Don't bother with the gun. You've already tried that

once and failed,' the colonel said, tapping the watch in his waistcoat.

'What are you going to do?'

'That depends on your clothes. Do they contain any Nylon?'

'No.'

'Good. Wouldn't want you to end up naked in the middle of the Peabody.'

'We're going to Yale?'

'It's as good a place to start as any. My sources tell me Benjamin Tallmadge met Nathan Hale there in 11.753.'

'When?'

'Sorry, I forget to use the temporal context — 1753. Although, I think before we try anything too ambitious, let's see how you cope with a relatively small jump — a hundred years should do.'

The colonel grabbed Anderson's hand and the world span away.

10

YALE

[Yale University, Connecticut. Date: 1917]

Anderson's father had taught at Yale.

Regardless of his illness, he was still an Emeritus Professor of American Studies and History, and even though he couldn't remember his wife's name, he could still recall every major event of the American Revolution.

When they appeared in the library of the Peabody museum it was the middle of the night.

Anderson felt his stomach lurch and he fell onto his knees. The room was spinning wildly as his hangover went into overdrive.

'Drink this, quickly,' said the colonel, squatting down and handing him a hip flask.

The liquor was strong, like brandy, warming his throat as it went down. Anderson didn't care what it was, it worked. He stood up as he felt the nausea subside.

He'd visited the museum a few times, but he didn't recognize the room that they'd appeared in. 'This isn't the Peabody.'

'It is, the building you know wasn't built until 11.925. This is the original, opened to the public in 11.876. Unfortunately, this one is about to be demolished for the Harkness Memorial Quadrangle.'

Anderson's father was a fellow of Saybrook College and had encouraged his son to go to Yale — like his sister was supposed to. As an act of rebellion Anderson had chosen Harvard, and his dad had never forgiven him.

They were in a long storeroom on the top floor of the building. The shelves were stacked with hundreds of old, leather volumes. Dusty glass display cabinets held the fragile skeletons of small dinosaurs like bone puppets on fine wires. Larger fossils were tagged with yellowing labels and stacked along the rafters of the roof.

'The collection of Othniel Charles Marsh,' the colonel explained, tapping on the glass. 'One of the most prolific paleontologists of the Bone Wars of 11.877, or at least he was until it bankrupted him.'

'What year?'

The colonel smiled. 'We use the Holocene Calendar: a system that begins ten thousand years further back than the Gregorian. So, 1877 becomes 11.877, it makes it a lot easier to navigate when you don't have to go into the negative.'

'You can travel back twelve thousand years?'

'Actually, we can go back further, but things get a little messy. Finding man-made objects that aren't entirely organic becomes harder. No one likes weaving with naturals, stone especially has a tendency to take you places you can't get back from even with a tachyon. Which reminds me,' he said, taking out another watch and strapping it onto Anderson's wrist.

'Is it a time machine?' Anderson asked, inspecting the watch.

'More like a tracker, think of it as a temporal GPS. There are only two things you really need to remember. This one,' he said, pointing at the first button, 'Takes you back two minutes. While this one will return you to a specific point in time. You can use it to bookmark other locations, but by default it returns you to the minute after you left the present.'

Anderson inspected the watch. His finger hovering over the second button. 'So I could just press this and go back home?'

'Just like the ruby slippers, Dorothy. But I don't think you will. This is one of those once in a lifetime opportunities that you've always secretly wished would happen.'

He looked up at the old man. 'You're telling me we just jumped back a hundred years.'

The colonel nodded to the window. 'Take a look outside.'

The buildings of the college were still recognizable, but also different, and the students looked like they'd just stepped out of an F. Scott Fitzgerald novel.

'It's okay, you'll get used to it,' the colonel said, patting him on the shoulder. 'The first hundred years are the hardest. Concepts like today, tomorrow and yesterday tend to blur into each other until it all just becomes about the "Now". Once you stop thinking like a linear you'll find it's quite liberating.'

'A linear?'

The old man tapped on the glass. 'Like them, people who travel toward the future, one day at a time.'

Anderson tried to make sense of what was happening, but his brain was refusing to accept what his eyes were seeing.

'I don't get it. We've just travelled a hundred years through an old box?'

'No, the box just provides a map. I followed its history to this room. We call them vestiges — like a bookmark. It appears to have been stored here for quite some time.'

'This shouldn't be possible. Did we fall through a wormhole or something?'

'There are far better men than me who could explain the "how". What you should be more concerned about is the "why".'

'So why are we here?'

The colonel walked towards the door. 'Yale has collected rare artefacts and books from civilizations all over the globe. The Antiquarians have established a base here in the museum, while the Scriptorians are running the library. I need to speak to them about a certain vestige that could get us back to 11.776.'

Anderson looked confused. 'These are other members of your Order?'

The colonel nodded. 'They're guilds within our Order. Antiquarians are responsible for precious artefacts, lost treasures and the like — most museums are run by them. While Scriptorians specialize in the collection of knowledge: forgotten books and manuscripts mostly. We're looking for the head librarian. If I remember correctly it's a man by the name of Keogh.'

11

LINONIAN

[College Library, Yale. Date: 1917]

The library was like a church. During his father's tenure it was known as Dwight Hall because by then all the books had been moved into the Sterling building.

Apparently, the architect was inspired by King's College Chapel in Cambridge, England. The central hall was vast, over fifty feet high, with carved arched columns that led off into tall stacks of books.

Anderson followed the colonel as he marched down the center of the nave carrying himself with the air of a visiting professor, which meant he was ignored by most of the librarians who were too busy returning books to their rightful places.

He headed directly for the reading rooms of the Linonian Society.

His father used to talk about the Linonian, which along with the Brothers in Unity, was one of the oldest secret societies within the college. One of Washington's spies, Nathan Hale, had belonged to it.

Keogh was a smart-looking gentleman in a three-piece suit and tie, who was overseeing the re-indexing of the Linonian library in the East Wing. He acknowledged the colonel with a nod as they entered the room before politely dismissing his assistants.

Keogh shook the colonel's hand. 'Westinghouse,' he said with a wry smile. 'What brings you to the twentieth?'

'Tempus edax rerum,' replied the colonel.

Time, devourer of all things. Anderson translated, wondering if it was some kind of password.

'Indeed it does. What can I do for you? I assume this isn't a social visit.'

'Anderson and I need to get back to the Culper ring,' he explained. 'We'd be interested to see the codebooks of Major Tallmadge or Sackett.'

Keogh frowned. 'When exactly are you trying to get to?'

'New York, 11.776.'

The librarian raised an eyebrow. 'Seventy-six may be difficult. The Culper ring wasn't established until seventy-eight and the codebooks weren't used until late seventy-nine or even eighty,' he said, walking over to a long display cabinet.

Anderson could see a set of old notebooks, buttons and other revolutionary memorabilia sitting in the soft black velvet of the display.

Keogh took out a small brass key and unlocked the cabinet. 'Major Tallmadge and Hale were here until 11.753. Since Hale was a member of the Linonian Society we have always maintained a small exhibit of their work. The late seventeen-seventies was a difficult time for artefacts: not just because of the Great Fire, so many of the spies' early communications were burned after reading, or intercepted by the head of British Intelligence, George Beckwith.'

After putting on a pair of cotton gloves, Keogh took out a notebook, its pages browned and stained with age. 'This is one of the only copies remaining — it'll get you back to 11.780.'

Anderson could see the pages of handwritten text, each word copied down in neat copperplate into ruled columns like an old accounting book. A number was assigned to every line, he scanned down the list until he found 711.

'Gen. Washington.'

The librarian closed the book and handed it to Westinghouse. 'I trust you will be needing more suitable attire.'

'You know me, I like to travel light.'

Keogh looked unimpressed. 'Follow me.'

He walked towards a tall wall of books and pulled out a tiny volume of poetry. The entire stack slid away to reveal a room of authentic-looking uniforms and weapons from the War of Independence.

'Please take care of the book and give my best to Culper Jr.'

12

PATRIOTS

The colonel browsed through the racks of clothes and picked out a blue jacket, white waistcoat and breeches.

'These should match Tallmadge's regiment,' he said, handing them to Anderson.

'You're serious?'

The old man narrowed his eyes. 'I assumed you wanted to come. Now that I've proved I'm not crazy.'

Anderson wondered what his father would say if he could see him now. The last time he'd had to dress up like a patriot was the Independence Day party of 1999. Now he was about to change into the outfit of a Washington memorial tour guide and use one of Tallmadge's codebooks to jump back to 1780.

Westinghouse wandered behind another rack of uniforms and was busy changing. 'The key thing is to try and blend in when we get back there. New York is on a knife edge. The British have captured the city and strangers are viewed with extreme suspicion. We'll have to infiltrate Tallmadge's camp and find something that can take us back another four years.'

Anderson took off his clothes, including his underwear — the colonel insisted that he couldn't take anything back. The material of his costume felt authentic, which was another way of saying it was itchy and uncomfortable. It smelled like it had never been washed, and there was even a stain on the breeches which he thought looked a little like blood.

The colonel appeared from behind the rail. His hair was tied back and stuffed underneath a tricorne hat, and he wore a long blue coat with white facings and beige breeches. He had gold epaulets on each shoulder and a red sash around his waist.

'I thought we weren't trying to stand out?' Anderson said.

The old man selected a gold handled sabre and strapped it on. 'Colonels tend not to be questioned, it's the privilege of rank. You're my adjutant. There has to be some sense of superiority between us.'

'Which is exactly why we kicked you out!'

'Hmm. I'm not trying to be an apologist for the British, but it does seem that you've managed to create a class society of your own. From my experience, civilizations always tend towards a two-class system: the privileged few taking advantage of the poor and disenfranchised, whether it's a monarchy or a republic.'

The colonel opened the codebook and put it onto the lectern in the middle of the room. He placed his hand on a page and closed his eyes. The lines of energy unraveled just as they had with his father's fossil case.

'Put your hand on the page,' he ordered.

13

1780

[Westchester County. Date: September 23, 1780]

The camp was a hive of activity. The local militia had captured a British spy and the news had everyone excited. Major Tallmadge had already ridden to Army headquarters in Tappan to dissuade Lieutenant Colonel Jameson, the post commander, from sending his prisoner on to General Arnold. Which meant that Tallmadge's tent was empty when they appeared inside it. He'd left in such a hurry that his writing desk was still covered in the notes and orders of the day.

Anderson knew it was Major John André, who'd been caught with the plans to West Point tucked into his stockings. He was traveling as a civilian under the name of John Anderson, which Anderson's father had always taken great pleasure in reminding his son about whenever he got the chance.

The colonel ignored the notes, opened Tallmadge's trunk and began to rifle through it.

Anderson went over to the desk.

'What are we looking for?'

'Tallmadge was very good friends with Nathan Hale. He's been dead for four years but I'm guessing the good Major would keep his old friend's correspondence with him.'

He pulled out a bundle of papers tied with a ribbon.

'All we need now is one of his last messages,' he said, handing the codebook and the letters to Anderson. 'Look for anything with a date close to the end of September 1776.'

'And what exactly are you going to do?'

The colonel picked up one of Tallmadge's small glass vials. 'The Culper ring had more than one method of enciphering their messages. This is invisible ink, or Sympathetic Stain as Doctor Jay would call it. I can use it to find Culper Jr, Robert Townsend. He owes me some money.'

And with that he disappeared.

Anderson stared in astonishment at the air where the colonel had stood. He couldn't believe that he'd just been dumped in the middle of a camp full of patriot soldiers who were on high alert for spies.

He took out the tachyon and his thumb stroked the second button. This time he'd be ready to jump.

His hand was shaking as he went through Hale's letters. He didn't read above the date at the bottom of the page, it felt too much like an intrusion. The words of a dead man were nothing but ink compared to the history he felt emanating from the paper.

Finally, he found a letter dated the 20th September, 1776. Hale had written to his old friend from New York. The content of the message was mostly recollections of their time together at Yale and how he was looking forward to returning home once the war was over. In the last paragraph he mentioned that the British had landed at Kips

Bay and that he planned to leave them with nothing but ashes.

Voices were raised outside, and Anderson quickly hid the letter within his coat and put the others back in the trunk.

'Stand aside,' barked the unmistakable voice of the colonel. The men obviously did as they were told as he came marching into the tent. He had a cut above his eye.

'Bloody tachyon's on the blink. I just appeared on the other side of the camp. Luckily the sentry was a terrible shot.'

Anderson handed him the letter.

The colonel read it and smiled when he got to the last paragraph. 'Seems we were right about Hale's intentions. Shall we take a look at that fire?'

14

FIRE

[New York Island. Date: September 22, 1776]

New York was on fire.

Flames were lighting up the sky, like the Fourth of July, and the heat from the blaze warmed their cheeks as they watched the inferno.

They'd appeared down by the quayside near Whitehall slip to find British marines running along the docks pulling handcarts filled with barrels of water. Residents were running in the other direction with everything they could carry.

'There's nothing quite as mesmerizing as a city on fire. History literally being erased before our very eyes,' said the colonel, his expression glazing over for a moment. 'Anyway, we're looking for the Fighting Cocks tavern,' he added, taking out his journal.

Anderson stared out at the fleet of British warships standing in the bay, tall sailing ships flying Union flags, their hulls bristling with cannons.

'Wasn't Hale captured in Queens the night before?'

'He was, but I suspect from his letter, that he may have had something to do with this.' He started walking towards the blaze.

When they turned onto Broadway they found the whole west side of Manhattan on fire. The city was mostly abandoned and many of the boarded-up, wooden buildings were empty. The air was full of smoke, and Anderson watched as the wind blew glowing embers along the shingled roofs setting them alight.

It was eerily quiet. No alarm bells were ringing, they'd all been melted down for cannons.

Ahead of them the tower of Trinity Church burned like a beacon all the way up its hundred-and-forty-foot steeple.

The tavern was directly ahead of them, a smoldering blackened ruin where the firefighters had damped it down and moved on.

The colonel moved aside as a detachment of Hessians, German mercenaries working for the British, ran past, carrying sacks of silver plate and various looted treasures from the ransacked houses of merchants.

'We need to move back a day, they'll start rounding up strangers soon,' the colonel said, kicking over the charred contents of the burned-out tavern.

Anderson looked around at the chaos, he was still having a problem believing he was actually standing in New York surrounded by the British Army.

15

FINDING NATHAN HALE

[Fighting Cocks tavern. Date: September 21, 1776]

The tavern was full of the drunk and debauched; off-duty soldiers and mercenaries groping prostitutes while playing cards for their stolen prizes, all of whom were oblivious to their arrival.

The colonel made for the bar and bought them both a tankard of rum.

Anderson needed a drink; his body was crying out for alcohol. He had no idea how long he'd gone without booze, but he gulped it down, trying hard not to cough as the rough liquid burned his throat.

He ordered another.

Anderson hadn't really thought about money, he'd assumed that it came with the costume. When he dug his hands into the inside pockets of his jacket he found a purse of coins, but the colonel stopped his hand before he took them out.

'Better not take that out in here,' he whispered.

They found a table in one corner of the rowdy bar and sat down.

'Currency is a little fluid here,' the colonel explained, 'and if I'm not mistaken you're probably carrying Continental Dollars rather than Pound Sterling.'

'Why are you trying to get to Hale?' Anderson asked hoarsely.

The colonel's eyes were scanning the room. 'Orders,' he said, tapping his notebook.

'Would you mind telling me what these orders are exactly?'

The colonel took a large swig of his drink and wiped his beard with his sleeve. 'No one knows how the fire started. Washington denied that the patriots had anything to do with it. There is a high probability that if I can save Captain Hale it may lead to the prevention of Washington's assassination.'

'How high?'

'The Copernicans latest estimate is sixty-five-point-two. There are more digits but they're hardly significant to anyone but them.' The colonel shrugged and held up the pages of his journal. Anderson saw a complicated set of flow diagrams and symbols animating across the paper.

'Nathan Hale could be the pivot on which the fate of the world turns.' The old man took another swig of the rum. 'Although there's a gentleman over there who would beg to differ.'

Anderson followed the colonel's gaze. A desperate group of soldiers were drinking and telling stories in one corner, one man kept looking over towards them.

'Colonel Robert Rogers himself.'

. . .

At that moment a tall man walked in. He was dressed like a school teacher with a burn scar on one side of his face. He was carrying a leather sack slung over one shoulder.

'That's Hale.' The colonel nodded. 'Stands out like a priest in a whore house.'

'What are you going to do?'

'What any good patriot would do of course. Keep your eye on him.' He stood up and walked towards Rogers.

The Queen's Rangers were a surly group of mercenaries that had been recruited from the Black Brigade and other loyalist units from Westchester and Long Island.

'Governor Rogers?' asked the colonel.

Rogers looked up from his cards. 'That's a title I haven't heard for a while. And who might you be?'

'Rufius Westinghouse, I was hired by Carver to look for the Northwest Passage.'

Rogers's eyes narrowed, they were red-rimmed, and his cheeks were flushed as if he'd been drinking all day. 'Well, you failed. As did Gage when he tried to send me down for treason.'

'And now you're fighting for the British?'

Rogers raised his glass. 'I fight for whoever has the coin to pay me.'

'Then let me buy you a drink.'

Anderson watched the colonel as he blocked Rogers's view of the room. Nathan Hale spoke briefly to the gruff-looking barman and handed over the satchel before turning and leaving.

While the colonel kept the ranger occupied, Anderson

took it upon himself to find out what was in the satchel.

A waitress was having a problem with one of the customers who'd mistaken her for a prostitute, as she untangled herself from the grip of the lecherous soldier the barman came out to help, leaving the bag unattended on the side.

Anderson wandered over to the bar, which was nothing more than a couple of planks of wood laid on top of a bunch of old barrels.

The satchel sat on the side next to a stack of empty bottles. Anderson pulled it across the bar and lifted the flap.

His hand froze on the timing mechanism of the bomb. His training told him that the fuse was chemical, a vial of liquid wired to a clockwork timer, nothing too fancy. There was a whole bunch of roman candle style fireworks attached to it.

As he closed the bag he felt someone's hand on his shoulder.

'And what do we have here?' asked a rough Irish accent.

Anderson turned to see Colonel Rogers and his men surrounding him. Behind them, Westinghouse was signaling to him, telling him to use his tachyon.

Reaching for his watch, Rogers caught his hand and put a blade to his neck. 'We'll keep our hands where we can see them thank you.'

There was nothing he could do.

16

HMS JERSEY

[Wallabout Bay, New York]

There was nowhere to sit below decks. The stench of a thousand men crammed into the old hulk of the ship was enough to make anyone gag. Most of the prisoners were naked, the heat was so intense in the cramped conditions that it made clothes unbearable. As Anderson was dragged past them he could hear the moans of the sick and dying, as well as the prayers of those who knew they were never getting out of this place alive.

He'd spent the last day aboard *HMS Eagle*, being questioned by Colonel Rogers and a British officer called De Lancey. They'd wanted to know who'd made the fire bomb, parts of which were scattered across the table in front of him.

After hours of relentlessly repeating the same set of questions, De Lancey changed tack and started asking him where he was from and what he was doing with such a fancy watch. When he refused to tell them, the interrogation got physical. Rogers was a big man, and his fists were like hammers. Anderson passed out a couple of times before De Lancey persuaded him to stop.

'We know there are more patriot spies in New York,' De Lancey said to the Rogers. 'Your job is simply to find them, mine is to decide what happens to them next.'

'Hang him and be done with it!' spat the ranger, putting the tachyon in his pocket. 'I'll be on my way.'

Compared to the ranger, De Lancey looked the epitome of a British officer. His uniform was spotless, the gold buttons glistened on his red jacket, and his white waistcoat and breeches showed no sign of battle. But there was something behind his eyes that told Anderson he was more dangerous than Rogers.

'You know we hang spies,' De Lancey said, examining the remnants of the incendiary device. 'Arsonists, however, could be argued to be more of a civil case. My guess is that you are nothing more than a delivery boy, a small link in the chain. Whoever started the fire last night had planned it very well. Multiple incendiaries, no alarm bells and a complete lack of usable firefighting equipment has left us with the west half of Broadway burned to the ground. Washington denies it of course, so what I need from you is simply the name of the man who gave this to you.'

Anderson ran his tongue along his teeth, some of them were loose and he could taste blood. He racked his memory for a character from the stories his father used to tell when he was a kid, and then it came to him.

'My name is John Anderson, I'm a clerk to Hercules Mulligan.'

De Lancey looked astonished. 'The tailor?'

Anderson nodded.

'He's a good man, finest stitching I've ever seen.' He

pulled down the sleeves on his jacket as if to show off the work in a better light.

'I was just given the package to take to the tavern. I had no idea what it was for.'

'By Mulligan?'

'No.' Anderson shook his head. 'By one of his clients.'

De Lancey's eyes widened. 'Are you saying this was instigated by a British Officer.'

Anderson nodded. 'Colonel Benedict Arnold.'

After that De Lancey had sent him to *HMS Jersey*, one of the prison ships moored out in the harbor.

Transferring him to the ship was Anderson's worst nightmare. His fear of water was not appreciated by the guards who accompanied him. They laughed when he refused to get in the jolly boat and knocked him out with the butt of one of their muskets.

He woke on the deck of the prison ship, looking up into a darkening sky as night fell. It was the 22nd September, the fire was out, and Nathan Hale was probably dead. Anderson had no idea where Westinghouse had gone and without the watch he had no way of getting back to the present.

The guards picked him up roughly and took him down into the hold.

17

DROWNING

The nightmare was always the same. He would wake up with the water rushing into the car. It was so cold that his hands had gone numb.

The seatbelt was jammed, and the water in his eyes blurred his vision, making it impossible to see what he was doing. His sister was slumped against the wheel, her face slowly disappearing below the surface and her blood turning everything red.

He couldn't breathe, he couldn't move. There was nothing he could do.

Then suddenly Candice was there, her fingers on the buckle and he was free.

The pressure of the car sinking pushed him out through the windscreen, and suddenly he was rising towards the glistening surface.

Anderson woke up with a gasp, as if he'd been holding his breath, only to find that the nightmare wasn't over. He was still trapped in the belly of an old ship, rough wooden planks against his back and rats crawling across his legs.

'They come when you're sleeping,' said the prisoner next to him. 'Takes those who don't fight back.' He kicked at one and sent it flying across to the other side of the hold.

'The Lord has forsaken us,' ranted another. 'There's nothing but damnation!'

Bilge water slopped around his feet, mixed with human waste it reeked like a stagnant cesspool. Anderson retched, but there was nothing left in his stomach. His throat was parched and his lips were dry. Water and food were left in barrels in the middle of the boat. Men fought over the scraps as he made his way over to it.

Suddenly the sound of cannons boomed out across the bay and the drummers beat to quarters. The guards rushed up onto the upper deck to see what was happening.

'I've been hit!' said one of the men standing up and pointing to the hull.

They watched as the end of a drill bit screwed up through the planking, it was followed by several more until a small circle had been cut out of the wood.

The center of the circle flew backwards, and the colonel's head appeared through it.

'Anderson?' he shouted, peering into the gloom.

Anderson couldn't find the words and just fell down on his knees before him.

'Quickly, get in the sub,' the colonel ordered.

18

THE TURTLE

The *Turtle* was a submersible developed by David Bushnell. Anderson recognized it from the model that his father used to keep on his desk.

The colonel had bored a hole just above the waterline. The rotting timbers of the hull weren't protected by the copper sheathing and had been easy to cut through. Anderson fell through the opening and into the dark water of the bay.

It was cold, like the lake, and he began to lose the feeling in his legs. He swam weakly towards the half-opened shell of the sub. He'd never been a strong swimmer, even before the accident and the current seemed to be pulling him away from the reach of the colonel.

'Come on lad,' said the old man. 'Before we catch our deaths.'

Anderson saw others falling out of the breach and swimming away. He knew the guards would soon see their escape and raise the alarm.

He kicked hard, willing his numb legs to move, driving himself forward towards the colonel's outstretched hand.

. . .

Anderson was shivering in the bottom of the submersible, too relieved to care that he was underwater. The *Turtle* was an egg-shaped wooden capsule that was powered by a system of gears hooked up to the pedals of a bicycle. Westinghouse was sweating as he frantically pedaled away from the boat. His head was stuck in the small, round conning tower, which sat above the waterline and a small snorkel arrangement mounted on it allowed them to breathe fresh air.

'Brilliant man, Bushnell. He was planning to use this to plant a bomb on *HMS Eagle,* Admiral Howe's flagship, but his pilot couldn't attach it. So, I convinced them to let me have a go. Although I'm not sure I've done much damage to the *Eagle*, it was a good enough diversion for what I needed to do.'

He didn't really understand what the old man was saying, he couldn't believe he was still alive. 'What happened to Hale.'

The colonel's voice grew somber. 'While I was saving you, Rogers captured Captain Hale. This mission has been aborted — I have orders to bring you back to base.'

'Where?'

'The Copernicans want a debriefing, but I think perhaps we should make a detour to Bedlam and have Doctor Crooke give you a once over. Just to make sure you haven't caught yourself a dose of cholera or worse.'

What on earth could be worse? thought Anderson.

19

BEDLAM

[Bethlem Hospital. Date: 1615]

Anderson thought they'd gone to the wrong century when he appeared in the sanatorium of Bedlam; Doctor Helkiah Crooke's med bay looked more like a medieval torture chamber than a physician's consulting room.

The doctor was bent over a cadaver, its chest opened up to expose the major organs. Crooke was making careful notes onto an anatomical illustration of the lungs.

'It's for his Mikrokosmographia,' the colonel whispered. 'It's a work of anatomical genius, at least a thousand pages and Shakespeare's printer is going to produce it — assuming that the Bishop of London doesn't ban it for showing women's genitalia.'

Anderson's head was pounding, and the brandy that the colonel had given him was wearing off. He sat down heavily on the examination table and let Crooke's nurse, who looked more like a nun, undress him.

Westinghouse sucked air through his teeth when he saw

the purpling on Anderson's ribs. 'Rogers certainly knows where to land his punches.'

'Yeah.'

'Why didn't you use your tachyon?'

'I didn't have time. I think he thought I was going for a gun.'

The colonel laughed. 'More like a knife. The guns of that era are a little too large to fit inside one's jacket. Where is it by the way?'

Anderson winced as the nurse placed a hot poultice against the side of his chest and wound a bandage around it. 'What?'

'Your tachyon?'

'They took it. Rogers stole it while De Lancey wasn't looking.'

The colonel scratched his beard. 'Did he now?'

Doctor Crooke put down his work, cleaned his hands and walked over to them. He wore a long black robe and stooped slightly, hunching his shoulders. Anderson couldn't think of a less appealing image for a physician, he looked more like a child-catcher.

'Looks like you've been wrestling a bear,' he said, examining Anderson's jaw and teeth.

'More like Mike Tyson.'

Crooke looked at the Colonel, who shrugged.

'I've a tincture that will soothe most of the damage to the face. The ribs will take longer, but nothing that shouldn't be right within an hour or so.

He walked over to shelves stacked high with bottles and jars, and began to put various dried powders into a mortar. 'I take it this is another one of your hare-brained missions

Rufius? The man is clearly not of the Order, does the founder even know he's here?'

'Not exactly,' answered Rufius looking slightly sheepish. 'The Copernicans have sanctioned the mission, but I encountered a few minor deviations.'

'Hmm,' the doctor murmured, grinding the medicine into a paste with a pestle. 'Open.' He took a wooden spatula and scooped some of it out onto Anderson's tongue.

It tasted terrible, like putrefied dead things boiled in the bilge water from the prison ship.

'Don't swallow,' Crooke warned, as Anderson pulled a face. 'It needs to be kept on the tongue for at least ten minutes. Marjorie the ten-glass if you please.'

Anderson thought he was going to throw up. The nurse went to a long line of hour-glasses and picked out one marked with the Roman numeral 'X'.

Rufius was incapable of standing still for ten seconds let alone ten minutes. He excused himself and left. Crooke went back to his anatomical drawings and the nurse simply smiled and left to attend to her other patients.

He could hear their screams echo down the corridor. They were the sounds of the insane.

20

TIMELINES

[Copernican Hall]

Two hours later, Crooke took the bandages off and inspected his ribs, the bruising was gone.

'How?' asked Anderson as he touched the skin.

'Temporal medicine,' said the colonel, walking back into the room. 'Accelerates the healing process a thousand-fold — smells like bat-shit though.'

'Out!' demanded the doctor waving his hand.

The colonel helped Anderson down from the table. 'I think we've outstayed our welcome,' he whispered, handing him a shirt.

They left Bedlam through a door that transported them straight into the central hall of the Copernican headquarters. The old man called it 'The Grand Nexus'. Like a shopping mall, it was long and narrow with a cathedral-like nave. Sunlight filtered down through a vaulted, stained-glass ceiling scattering rays of ruby, topaz and emerald over the crowd. Anderson could see hundreds of floors on each side with massive gears and clockwork components filling every available space — it made him feel like he was inside a giant antique clock.

Bells chimed from the far end of the hall and he turned to see an enormous rotating dial made up of concentric rings inscribed with numerals and symbols. Everyone around him took out their own timepieces and checked them, before going back to their work.

Hundreds of men and women in richly-colored robes crossed the concourse. They were all busily adjusting complicated abacuses or flicking through thick books. An old man with a long white beard walked by, tossing a coin repeatedly and calling out 'naive' or 'caput' to a young boy who followed behind, keeping tally on a beaded rope.

'Copernicans are obsessed with random,' explained the colonel. 'Standard random coefficients are tested every century or so to ensure they're compensated correctly.'

'Using the Bernoulli process,' said Anderson.

'Indeed,' said a tall, thin man who'd appeared beside the colonel, he looked impressed.

'Anderson, this is Professor Eddington.'

The professor nodded to him. 'Welcome Mr Anderson. Rufius tells me that you have a masters in mathematical cryptography. Perhaps you would care for a tour of our difference engine?' He raised his hand up across the floors and Anderson realized that the whole building must be one giant machine.

There was a look in the colonel's eye, and a slight shake of the head that told him it was a bad idea.

'I'd love to but —'

'Won't we be late for the simulation?' interrupted the colonel.

'Of course, data analysis has already prepared the scenario. Follow me.'

The data analysis room had a domed ceiling illuminated by a spherical projector installed in the center of the floor, it reminded Anderson of the Hayden Planetarium.

'Primary sequencing has been completed on the vestige,' one of the members of the professor's team advised, as he walked in with Anderson and the colonel in tow.

'Since the failure of the Hale scenario, we used the object you retrieved from Yale to examine other options.' Eddington pointed to the codebook that sat in a glass cylinder beneath the projector. 'We should now be able to compute the next statistically viable intervention. Simeon, the program if you please.'

A young man took out a large stack of white cards from a velvet lined wooden box and placed them on a shelf at the base of the brass projector.

He pulled a lever and the cards descended into the bowels of the machine, lights illuminated the glass floor beneath their feet. Thousands of gears turned through hundreds of different combinations a second, processing the punched cards.

The noise of the machinery drowned their voices, but Anderson could see Eddington giving instructions to his team using a complicated form of sign language.

A light flared inside the central projector and streams of data were beamed out onto the surface of the dome above them. They watched as thousands of branching lines and symbols flashed across its surface, too fast to be read.

At the center of the hemisphere was a date, the number descending rapidly as the search ran back through time. He watched the digits crawl slowly back towards 11.776. As it reached the relevant year the display began to slow, shifting and scaling as the engine focused in on its subject.

Then it stopped, and the noise lowered to a hum.

There in the center of a cluster of glyphs was Washington's timeline, a finely traced network of connecting variables, factors and a thousand other things that influenced his life.

'Could you expand nexus two-delta,' asked the colonel, squinting at one area of the ceiling.

Eddington's team pulled a series of levers and the projection zoomed into the cluster. The finer details separated out, unpacking themselves to create a cloud of events and people.

'Who is that?' asked Anderson, his analytical mind beginning to see the patterns in the web of events.

'One of the conspirators, David Matthews,' answered Eddington. 'The Mayor.'

'And him?' Anderson pointed to another cluster of activity.

'William Tryon, Governor of New York.'

'So, where's Thomas Hickey?'

'The assassin? We're having difficulty connecting him, we still need more data to work with,' Eddington said, moving the focus of the display to show Hickey's timeline, it ended the day after Washington's.'

'And you seriously believe Washington should have survived?'

'Indeed we do, but what we don't know is when exactly the deviation took place,' answered the colonel.

The professor nodded. 'It's imperative that we find the

inciting incident, if we initiate an amendment too early in the chronology we risk irreparable damage to the continuum. We don't have enough data from the period to know exactly how it was changed.'

'But we do have a very good idea what happens if it continues on its current trajectory,' said the colonel.

Eddington gestured to one of his assistants, and the map zoomed out and lines began to spread out from the point where Washington had been killed. He walked out onto the floor and pointed to an area of red lines. 'As you can see, our calculations predict a seventy-three per cent probability of divergence at 11.917. The United States was restricted by the Franklin directives and wasn't able to join the allies against Germany, resulting in the defeat of the British and the creation of a German super state.'

Anderson studied the branching flow as dates and symbols rose and fell across the dome.

'You're saying if the US had been involved they could have won the Great War?'

Eddington nodded. 'Franklin's legal processes restricted Woodrow Wilson, keeping America out of the conflict — even after the Zimmerman telegram. The repercussions of this were extensive: no nineteenth amendment, no racial equality and certainly no Russian Revolution. A victory, on the other hand, would give America the confidence and patriotism that would make them leaders of the free world.'

'And Germany would never dominate Europe,' added the colonel. 'Even after the second attempt.'

'Wait, you're telling me that this plan of yours causes a second World War?'

The colonel grimaced. 'The lesser of two evils, I'm afraid.'

'I don't see how saving Washington makes things that much better?' Anderson pointed at the timeline.

Eddington switched off the projector. 'Because the rise of the United Federation of Germany will eventually lead to an atomic war with Russia. The nuclear winter will decimate the population. The planet will become uninhabitable.'

21

AUROCH

[Chapter House]

There was one man who knew the period better than anyone — his father.

'You cannot go back into your own timeline,' the colonel said, shaking his head.

'My dad was one of the most respected authorities on the war. If we go back to before I was born, he won't even recognize me.'

'It's one of the fundamental principles of our Order. You cannot interact with your own chronology — what if you stopped him from meeting your mother. The whole grandfather paradox takes months to repair and the paperwork is ridiculous.'

'But he won't trust you, and I know how he thinks. I can persuade him to help us.'

The colonel scratched his beard as he studied his almanac. All of the details from the timeline that Eddington had shown them were now copied down onto its pages, parts of which seemed to keep changing.

'It's too dangerous. My orders are to go back and find out more about the conspiracy. If we start digging around in your past, we'll end up alerting the Protectorate and you really don't want to get in their bad books believe me.'

'The Protectorate?'

The colonel grimaced. 'Time Police. A nasty bunch of fascists who take their job far too seriously — bit like the Stasi.'

'And who were they?'

'Never mind.'

The colonel had brought him to a 'Chapter House' in Brooklyn to recuperate before their next mission. The house was an unusual collection of rooms that seemed to exist in different parts of history, although from the outside it looked like any other brownstone building in Cobble Hill.

It was the first time Anderson had a chance to meet some of the other members of the Order. The house seemed to be a staging-post for the strangest bunch of people he'd ever seen from all over the last twelve thousand years.

'He knows everything about that era. I grew up listening to stories about Hale, Tallmadge and Sackett.'

'No. We still have to check up on Governor Tryon and Matthews, and find the link to Hickey.'

Anderson felt guilty about what had happened to Nathan Hale. He wasn't sure why they couldn't just go back and try again, but the colonel hadn't wanted to talk about it. There was something about the way he avoided the subject that made him think this wasn't the first time he'd failed to save someone. Anderson wondered how frustrating it must be to have the power to put something right and not act on it. All the colonel would say was that there were always consequences.

'They certainly know how to cook their beef here,'

Anderson said, changing the subject. He carved off a piece of steak and put it into his mouth.

'That's probably not beef,' said the colonel without looking up from his journal.

Anderson stopped chewing. 'What is it?'

'Depends what day it is.'

'I've no idea.'

The colonel took a bite of the meat from his own plate and laughed. 'Auroch. Probably a couple of thousand years old.'

'Tastes okay.'

'I'm sure it does, it was probably roaming the plains a few hours ago. One of the benefits of time travel... our game larder is pretty diverse.'

'So, you can bring things back from other times.'

'Without them ageing? There are ways, although the Antiquarians tend to leave their artefacts in storage. No one likes an antique that looks like brand new.'

'Does that include people?'

'No-one is allowed to bring a linear out of their timeline.'

'But you did that to me.'

'You have latent abilities, and you're from the present, the frontier.'

'I should probably get back there, they'll be wondering where I've got to.'

'That reminds me. Try not to lose this one,' the colonel said, handing him a new tachyon. 'You're still not quite grasping the concept of time travel are you? We could stay here for years and I can still get you back to the minute you left. No one knows you're missing.'

'So, what's the plan?' asked Anderson, strapping the watch to his wrist.

The colonel took out a few large banknotes that were tucked in the back of his journal and handed them to him. They were printed in a woodblock style with ornate borders and the words 'ONE THIRD OF A DOLLAR' in capital letters across the top and down the sides. It was dated February 17th, 1776 and signed by Johnson.

'This is what Townsend discovered,' explained the old man. 'Fake dollar bills. If Eddington's calculations are correct, Tryon is printing counterfeit currency and using it to bribe patriots to work for the British.'

'And that helps us how?'

'This may be the link we've been looking for, Hickey was caught with counterfeit currency.'

22

DUCHESS

[Duchess of Gordon. Date: June 29, 1776]

They stood on the docks looking out towards Staten Island. Dressed as merchants so as not to raise suspicion.

The colonel opened his almanac and turned to Eddington's algorithm. 'When the Continental Army moved into New York, Governor Tryon moved his headquarters to *HMS Duchess of Gordon*,' the colonel explained pointing at the intertwining lines.

Anderson looked out into the harbor, shuddering at the sight of the prison ships and the large warships that floated amongst them.

'I don't get it. If we know the exact location and time that Washington was killed, why don't we just go there and stop it?'

'As Eddington explained: knowing and acting are two very different things. If we adjust the timeline at the wrong moment we could initiate all sorts of unexpected consequences. What we don't know yet is how the plot should be foiled or who instigated it. The secret to being a good Watchman is finding the smallest fraction of change to deliver the best outcome. I need all the facts before I execute a course correction.'

'And you do this for a job?'

The colonel sighed. 'For as long as I can remember.'

'Why?'

'Because the future depends on it, the Order was formed to keep the human race on the right track.'

'And who decides that exactly?'

'Men with greater minds than you or I. They've been studying probability for so long it's become a science or in some cases, a religion. Ours is not to reason why and all that.'

He took out one of Townsend's fake dollar bills and Anderson watched as he opened its timeline.

They appeared below decks beside the makeshift printing press, which was nothing more than a simple set of wooden blocks with etched metal plates. Hundreds of Continental dollars hung from the wooden joists. Anderson estimated there must have been at least twenty grand drying above his head.

They made their way through the creaking ship and into the captain's quarters which was more like a floating office than a warship. Documents were piled up in corners of the cabin and there were maps and charts laid out across the large dining table.

'Troop movements,' noted the colonel. 'The patriots would be very keen to have five minutes with these.'

'And we'd be dead if anyone found us in here,' Anderson whispered, looking nervously at the door.

The colonel winked and began to search through the files on Tryon's desk. 'They're on deck, watching the arrival of Admiral Howe's fleet. The Governor does love a bit of ceremony.'

The ship pitched, and Anderson felt his stomach lurch. 'Remind me, what exactly are we looking for?'

'A link to Hickey or someone within his network that might have Patriot sympathies. I need an informer, anyone who would be close enough to Tryon, but not so enamored of the British.'

Anderson picked up a pistol. It was heavy compared with his Glock, and he wondered how much shorter the revolution would've been if the Patriots had used automatic weapons.

He could feel the history flowing beneath the patterned stock.

The colonel was rifling through a series of letters, his expression changing as he read them.

'There's something encrypted in these that involves Samuel Fraunces, the innkeeper, but I can't tell what. You're good with cyphers – take a look.'

Anderson ignored him. His fingers were tingling as the timeline of the pistol unraveled around his hand. He saw events like knots entwined into the ribbons of energy. The weapon had been used the night Washington died, he could feel the violence of the firefight and couldn't help himself, he was drawn into it.

'Drop it!' He heard the colonel shout, but it was too late.

23

ASSASSINATION

[Richmond Hill. Date: June 23, 11.776]

Anderson appeared in the trees close to Washington's headquarters at Richmond Hill.

The night was just as his father used to describe. A dark, star-filled sky hung over the road as General Washington rode ahead of his senior officers, all disguised as merchants. His bodyguards were following behind him in a covered wagon. The road was heavily rutted after the rain and the cart was being thrown around as they went.

From what Anderson could remember three of the men on the wagon were conspirators. Sergeant Hickey was a persuasive man and had used the counterfeit money Governor Tryon was printing to buy their loyalty.

The Hudson River was less than a hundred yards to their left. According to his dad, a Durham boat was moored just off shore with a unit of Rogers' Rangers dressed as farmers ready to take out Washington, the loyal members of his lifeguards and any senior officers that got in their way.

His heart was beating hard as he watched the party approach along the Greenwich Road.

The colonel appeared a minute later dressed as an officer from the Continental Army with a rifle in one hand and a pistol in the other. A bandolier was slung over one shoulder with a sabre hanging from his waist.

'So what part of subtle manipulation do you not get?' he asked Anderson, handing him the rifle.

Anderson would have preferred his Glock, but the old man had explained before that technology wouldn't make it back in one piece.

'I didn't mean to. The pistol just kind of opened up in my hand.'

'It's Gilbert Forbes, the gunsmith. I believe he was involved in supplying the weapon that killed Washington.'

They both ducked as a shot rang out from the trees behind them. The Rangers had landed, and the colonel put his finger to his lips and crept off into the undergrowth.

Anderson knew the attack was nothing but a diversion, the real danger was waiting in the wagon.

At the sound of the shot, Washington's officers circled their leader, taking out their guns and firing into the trees. The lifeguards scrambled out from the back of the wagon and Anderson saw the flash of their blue coats as they spread out across the road, shooting into the dark.

He saw one of the officers hang back as the others moved into position. Anderson guessed it must be Sergeant Hickey. With everyone focused on the enemy, all he had to do now was shoot Washington in the back.

Anderson sighted his Pennsylvania Rifle at Hickey's head, his marksman training at the academy had been with a more powerful AR-15 carbine, where a clean shot through the head meant less chance of any muscle spasm on a detonator. The inaccuracy of the gun he held against his cheek meant that he had a much better chance of success if he went for the chest.

Hickey raised his pistol.

Anderson fired.

The smoke burned into his nostrils and made his eyes water. He blinked back the tears and tried to clear his vision.

Hickey was down.

The other officers turned their guns on Anderson. Musket balls ripped through the foliage, taking chunks out of the tree trunks. He dropped the rifle and rolled away, crawling on his belly into the bracken.

When he reached a clearing, he saw the colonel fighting hand-to-hand with Rogers, five or six of his Rangers lay dead around them.

The clash of their swords was a hard and fierce sound in the night. The firing had stopped, and Anderson knew it would be a matter of seconds before the remaining lifeguards found them.

He stood up and Rogers spotted him.

The big man punched the colonel in the gut and raised his sword as if to take off his head.

A shot rang out from behind Anderson and hit Rogers in the shoulder knocking him backwards.

George Washington stepped out of the bushes, still holding the smoking pistol. It took Anderson a moment to realize that he'd actually saved him before Rogers shot the General between the eyes.

Anderson hit the second button on his tachyon.

24

CONSEQUENCES

[Greenwich Village, New York. Date: Wednesday, January 19, 2018]

He was back in his apartment.

There was pizza scattered all over the floor, and the clock read 06:05 — one minute after they'd left. The old man said that there was a one minute safety margin built in to stop you from meeting yourself.

Anderson sat down on the couch, everything looked the same. Isobel's stuff was still missing, and he wondered if anything had changed at all.

He grabbed his wallet from the counter and took out a dollar bill.

The note had a picture of Queen Elizabeth II and the signature of the Governor of the Bank of England.

'What the —'

Suddenly, two men in black armor appeared out of thin air and shot him in the chest with some kind of taser.

. . .

'This is what you get for working with a latent.'

Anderson's head felt like it had been hit by a train and his body was numb. The stranger's voice sounded far away, and distorted, like a bad phone connection.

'The whole point of the mission was to find a subtle way to save the man, not create another bifurcation.'

'He's young, and perhaps a little headstrong.'

He recognized the voice of the colonel, but kept his eyes shut and controlled his breathing.

'The Chief Inquisitor is demanding his redaction. Ravana has most of the council on her side.'

The colonel grunted. 'That's because they're all scared of her.'

'And what do you suggest we do with him?'

Anderson could feel his other senses returning. His arms were tied and there was something on his head, strapped under his chin like a helmet.

'Give him a chance to fix it. He does show a great deal of promise.'

'Yes, Eddington told me he grasped the basics of temporal mechanics immediately.'

The colonel sighed. 'He's a natural candidate for the Copernicans. I suspect our Professor would take him on in a heartbeat.'

'Not a Watchman then?'

'No, he's too impulsive, doesn't understand the nuances of the role.'

'Neither did you when you started.'

'This Washington deviation is a difficult mission. I would have struggled if it was my first time. Trying to find the right adjustment with limited data is proving to be a challenge.'

The stranger walked towards them, from the sounds of

his boots on the stone floor Anderson assumed they were in some kind of cell.

'I'll overrule the Protectorate, on the understanding that you work with the Grand Seer.'

'But —'

The stranger interrupted. 'The seers can provide valuable insights when factual information is scarce.'

'Kelly's as mad as a box of frogs.'

'He's the best we have.'

'No one knows that period better than my father,' said Anderson, opening his eyes.

25

DAD

[Yale University, Connecticut. Date: 1990]

His father's office looked exactly the same. It was nine years before Anderson was born, and a photograph of his ten-year-old sister sat in a silver frame on his desk.

There was a moment, when he'd introduced himself as John Bolton, that he thought he saw a glimmer of recognition in his dad's face, but it passed quickly.

No child should meet their parents before they were born. It was such a strange feeling to see his dad so positive and happy. He was at the peak of his career: a respected member of the history department with a book in the New York Times best sellers list.

There would be a few more successes before that tragic day arrived and the drinking started, before their family fell apart.

Anderson was nervous when he came to shake his father's hand in case the universe exploded.

But it didn't.

. . .

He'd told the faculty secretary that they were from the FBI, investigating a matter of national security. His old man loved any kind of conspiracy and devoured espionage books, especially ones about the War of Independence.

The colonel had insisted on coming along for the ride. Since the screw-up with the assassination he seemed more cautious, especially after the meeting with the founder.

Anderson only learned who the stranger was afterwards. The guy looked like an old wizard with the most piercing blue eyes. Rufius wasn't convinced it was a good idea to visit Anderson's father — complaining that there were at least ten other experts that they could use within the twentieth century, but the founder ignored him and gave it his blessing.

The colonel looked uncomfortable in a business suit, fiddling with his collar like a school kid about to have his photograph taken.

Anderson managed to hold it together when they walked into his father's office. His dad was so much younger than he remembered, more like the photos that they used to look through at Christmas and laugh over with their grandparents.

He started with the standard set of questions: about his dad's background and qualifications, watching him slowly lose the suspicious look in his eyes.

Then he let slip some details about the case. He kept the lie simple: a number of Washington's letters had been recovered during a fraud investigation and they were looking for someone to verify their authenticity.

His father's eyes narrowed, a sure sign he was interested. There was nothing more exciting than the discovery of new material for a historian, but they were a cautious bunch, pure-bred cynics to the core.

'What's the provenance?' he asked, leaning forward and placing his elbows on the desk.

'The Smithsonian are carbon dating them now.'

'Hah, really? I could have saved you the trouble,' he said with an air of arrogance. 'The eye is a far more capable judge than a machine.'

'I wanted to ask about Washington. The letters seem to contain details of a secret code.'

His father smiled. 'General Washington was the spymaster of the Culper ring. He was known as agent 711.'

Anderson feigned ignorance, knowing that this was one of his father's favorite topics.

'There were a lot of problems with messages getting intercepted. So-called 'Black Chambers' where communiques would be opened and read by the enemy before being sent on their way. Many couriers were double agents; encrypting the message became the only way to ensure its security.'

'So, these letters would have a cypher key?'

'Yes, they used codebooks, dictionaries of keywords and numerical references. I have one here in the library if you wish to see it?'

'No, thank you, sir. But would you be able to decrypt these for us?'

Anderson took out a photocopy of one of Tryon's letters that the colonel had found onboard the *Duchess*.

He took the letter. 'That depends on whether it uses one of the known lexicons.'

His father put on his glasses and stared at the pages for a few minutes before answering.

'This isn't Washington's handwriting.'

'It's not?' Anderson acted surprised.

'No, this is more like Governor Tryon.'

He got up from his desk and went over to the large collection of books stacked on the shelves behind him.

Anderson glanced at the colonel who looked impressed. His father had passed the first test.

'Yes. Tryon. Here's a note he wrote to London when they refused to land the tea at Boston:

> *"only under the protection of the point of the bayonet, and muzzle of cannon, and even then I do not see how consumption could be effected"*

The Committee of Safety believed Tryon was responsible for Washington's assassination, but it could never be proved.'

The colonel stopped fidgeting and sat forward. 'I don't understand why so little is known about that night?' he asked in a perfectly acceptable American accent.

'The assassination was not made public for over a week. Nathanael Greene took command of the Continental Army and since the British were massing on Staten Island, he had no time to waste. He had to get the Patriot troops out of New York. After Bunker Hill the British had realized the Continental Army had become a force to be reckoned with and had drafted in thousands of German mercenaries, which, with the help of the British Navy, were on their way south from Nova Scotia to take Manhattan.'

'How did Tryon recruit Hickey?'

'He used a gunsmith named Forbes. Hickey had been complaining about the impending British attack to his fellow officers for months. Tryon was printing counterfeit currency on the *Duchess of Gordon*, and Hickey was reprimanded for passing forged money. If this is a genuine letter from Tryon, I'd bet my last dollar on it being a communique to Hickey, Forbes or even the Mayor, David Matthews — they were all working together.'

Anderson stood up and took the letters back from his father.

'Thank you for your time.'

'I'm sorry I can't help you further. I doubt that you'll ever know what it contained, not without the mask.'

'Mask?'

'They used to cut shapes out of a paper sheet and lay it over the writing, leaving the words of the message to show through. It's simple but quite effective. I suppose one could try to decrypt it if you had enough patience.'

Anderson tried to remember what else had been on Tryon's desk, and he could tell the colonel was doing the same.

'We suspect that these letters were stolen from the Fraunces Tavern Museum,' said the colonel. 'Could they have something to do with Samuel Fraunces?'

'Well the Fraunces tavern was often used as a meeting place by the Continental Congress. Washington first had dinner there in April 1776 and would regularly order take-out. If Tryon was trying to persuade someone to poison Washington, Fraunces would be the guy, but I don't think that's likely.'

'Take-out?'

'Yes, Samuel Fraunces would use clay pots and seal the food with a layer of fat. He supplied the Commander while he was lodging at Richmond Hill.'

'So Fraunces would have direct access to Washington?'

'Yes, or at least his servants would.'

The colonel had obviously heard enough and stood up.

Anderson took one last look at the framed picture.

'Your daughter?'

'Yes. Candice.'

He wanted desperately to tell his dad not to take that flight, that it wasn't his fault she died, but he couldn't find the right words.

'We should be going,' warned the colonel.

26

FRAUNCES

[Fraunces Tavern, New York. Date: 2018]

The tavern was a three-story brick mansion, reconstructed to look like the original one that Samuel Fraunces had purchased from De Lancey in 1762 and named the 'Queens Head'.

Anderson's father had given the colonel an idea. Fraunces could be the perfect way to reach Washington, all they needed to do was plant the seed of the conspiracy in the innkeeper's head and let his sense of duty do the rest.

Anderson, on the other hand, saw it more as an opportunity to get a decent drink and some twenty-first century comforts.

The one thing that no one warned you about the past was that it smells like shit. It made him appreciate the simple things in life, like flushing toilets and deodorant, let alone dental hygiene.

. . .

The bar was buzzing; filled with a mixture of New Yorkers and tourists on the whiskey tour.

This was always Anderson's favorite time of day: that first golden hour after work, when everyone was winding down and meeting their friends, before the booze took over and the stories lost their shine.

They went over to the bar. People mistook their eighteenth-century costumes for those of tour guides and some of them insisted on taking selfies. Anderson smiled at how uncomfortable it made the colonel to be surrounded by crowds of Japanese tourists with cameras, but it was soon forgotten — when the first bottle came down off the shelf.

'Good whiskey,' said the old man, sampling the single malt.

'Fine German whiskey,' Anderson agreed, looking at the gothic label.

The colonel grimaced. 'That's never going to sound right.'

The second floor of the tavern had been restored to the original rooms that Washington and his officers would have used before the British arrived.

It had been turned into a museum with collections of framed letters and engravings hanging on the walls, each one with a neat label pinned underneath.

There was a wooden barrier separating the public from the exhibits. The colonel waited patiently until the coast was clear and then vaulted over it and made for one of the letters.

He disappeared before anyone noticed.

Ten seconds later he reappeared.

'Are you coming?'

. . .

[Fraunces Tavern, New York. Date: June 21, 11.776]

Compared to the Fighting Cocks, Fraunces Tavern was a high-class establishment.

Anderson could tell how far they'd travelled based on the lack of air conditioning, the clouds of pipe smoke and the scent of unwashed bodies that assailed his senses.

The colonel marched off down the corridor and Anderson followed him. Passing the long room, he recognized members of the Continental Congress busily eating oysters and talking over one another.

'This place positively exudes history,' said the colonel looking up at the hole where a cannon ball from *HMS Asia* had destroyed part of the roof. 'So many influential people have passed through its doors — the Sons of Liberty, the New York Congress and both British and Continental Commanders. This is what we call a causal nexus, a point in time where many lines intersect.'

They descended the stairs to the ground floor.

'How exactly is Fraunces going to help us?'

'I think Black Sam has his fingers in many pies — excuse the pun. We just need to find the right motivation to convince him that uncovering the conspiracy could work to his advantage. We need someone who can read him.'

'Like a profiler?'

The colonel laughed. 'No, I meant a seer.'

Anderson looked confused. 'A seer? A psychic?'

He shook his head. 'They're special. While we can read the timelines of objects, they can do the same to people. They can see what the future holds. It's an innate talent that they're born with — but it comes at a price, tends to make them a little crazy.'

'I resent that,' said a man, sitting in one corner of the tavern.

He was dressed like a pirate, with charms and ribbons woven into his wild hair. He wore a tricorn hat and a black leather coat that was studded with metal symbols that Anderson recognized from Eddington's data projection — temporal glyphs.

'Edward Kelly, as I live and breathe. What are you doing here?'

'The portents guided me,' Kelly replied, waving his hands in the air like a mystic.

'More likely the founder did,' the colonel muttered.

'Who is this odd fellow?' asked Kelly, his eyes focusing on Anderson.

'Nobody important.'

Kelly's fingers moved as if playing on some invisible instrument. 'Death hovers over him like a shadow, a cold, watery death.'

'Not now Edward,' warned the colonel.

Kelly got to his feet, the men at the other tables looked up from their card games.

'What's he doing?' whispered Anderson.

'He's a seer, they're attracted to traumatic deaths. I should keep your distance if I were you.'

The colonel got between them and sat Kelly down in his chair. 'You've got an audience Edward, I suggest you play the fool.'

'If I must.'

He covered his right hand with a handkerchief and then lifted it off with a dramatic flourish to reveal a raven. The onlookers took a deep breath and crossed themselves. Kelly put the bird on his shoulder and took a drink from his tankard.

'We could use your assistance,' the colonel said, once everyone had gone back to their games.

Kelly was breaking walnuts with his bare hands and feeding them to the raven. 'So I've been told.'

'I need you to read the owner of this establishment, Samuel Fraunces. Find out what he knows.' The colonel nodded towards a powdered-wigged man who was walking among his patrons.

'Stars, hide your fires; Let not light see my black and deep desires,' quoted the seer.

Kelly waited for the right moment and stood as Fraunces passed by. Pretending to be slightly worse for drink he caught the man by the arm and span him around to face him. Anderson saw Kelly's eyes darken as he took hold of the innkeeper's hand. Time seemed to slow as the seer looked deep into Fraunces's face, like a critic studying a piece of sculpture, looking for flaws in the work.

Thirty seconds passed and then it was over. Fraunces moved on as if he'd never met the man. Kelly slumped back down in the chair and took a long drink.

'Well?' demanded the colonel.

Kelly nodded. 'There's nothing more interesting than a man with a secret.'

'And?'

'There's a woman. A fallen woman. The fate of the nation turns around her,' he said, spinning a coin across the table.

'So it does,' agreed the colonel.

27

THE WOMAN

'So, one woman could change the entire course of the future?'

The colonel nodded, stuffing a clay pipe full of tobacco and lighting it. 'That's generally how it happens.'

Anderson thought about Isobel, how she had influenced the last two years. It wasn't something he'd planned on, but somehow, they'd slipped into a routine that became too comfortable to leave.

'Not a bullet then?' he said, remembering the firefight on Greenwich Road.

The colonel laughed. 'Those are the easy ones. Nice clean disruptions that you can stop with a defective fuse or diversion. The real skill comes from finding a subtle change, one that could take years to take effect.'

Like the pain I hid from her, Anderson thought, the one that burned slowly away at the foundations of their relationship until there was nothing left but the memory of what could have been.

'Love, Lust and Liberty,' Kelly proposed, holding up his tankard. It was obvious he was very drunk.

'Your friend is a few sheets to the wind.'

The colonel smiled. 'That's his normal state.' Then suddenly Kelly took the raven and threw it in the air. 'This however, is about to get very interesting.'

The bird exploded into a cloud of feathers and the bar came to a complete standstill, as if time was frozen.

The pirate got up and walked between the statue-like crowd. Like a puppet master he repositioned their limbs and hands into ridiculous poses, hopping from one foot to the other as he moved between them.

'Kelly, the woman!' the colonel reminded him.

The crazy man tipped his hat towards the colonel and danced around the room, stopping at the various serving girls until he found one woman in particular.

His eyes lit up as he touched her shoulder.

'Your prize,' he said with a bow and clicked his fingers.

The feathers turned to smoke and time restarted.

'What is your name?' asked the colonel.

'They call me Phoebe,' she replied nervously.

'Tell me Phoebe, have you spent much time with Sergeant Hickey of late?'

She looked down at the floor. 'I may have.'

The colonel took out a purse, heavy with coin, and dropped it onto the table.

'When you were pretending to sleep, did you perhaps overhear him discussing any interesting plans?'

She picked up the purse and weighed it in her hand. 'I told Master Fraunces, he said it weren't nothing but hearsay.'

'Quite right,' said the colonel snatching the purse out of her hands. 'You may go.'

'But —'

'Was there something else?'

'I might have caught a snippet of a thing, a name or two.'

The colonel smiled. 'Like Washington?'

She nodded.

'And?'

'And how they was going to take him on the Greenwich Road. Thomas is going to hand him to the Rangers.'

'Rogers' Rangers?'

There were tears in her eyes. 'Thomas said it would be for the best, as the British were going to win anyway, and we would all be heroes.'

'How the world turns on the toss of a coin,' added Kelly, rolling a coin across his knuckles. 'Once a hero, now a villain.'

The colonel gave her the purse. 'Go directly to Richmond Hill and tell General Putnam what you know.'

She curtsied and left.

'And that's all it takes,' he said, raising his tankard and turning to Anderson. 'One subtle change of behavior and mission accomplished!'

'How do you know they'll take her seriously?'

The colonel opened his almanac and handed it to Anderson. 'Look for yourself. I can already feel the timeline shifting.'

The lines that crawled across the old man's almanac were redrawing themselves as he watched, new branches and symbols rose and fell across the page, moving through time as the effects of the change stabilized.

'The future just got brighter,' the colonel said proudly, tapping the relevant point in the diagram.

28

THE ACCIDENT

[Greenwich Village. Date: Wednesday, January 19, 2018]

Anderson held the St Christopher medallion in the palm of his hand, his thumb brushing against the contours of the engraving.

His father had given it to him on his seventh birthday, and he remembered how it had made him feel like a super-hero, invincible.

But the patron saint of travelers and sudden deaths hadn't come through for him on that day. The medics had taken it off in the hospital before he went into the MRI, and he'd never been able to put it back on since.

He could still see the silver chain glinting in the water as he floated up towards the surface, his oxygen-starved brain imagining it was taking him up towards heaven.

Now, standing in his empty apartment he wondered if it might have a use after all.

Opening the timeline, he let its chronology weave out

around his arm. Fine lines of the past coalesced into a pattern, a map of his childhood.

And there in the middle of the limited timeline was the worst day of his life.

It took everything he had to open that event.

The snow was deep on the bend and he could see where her car had left the road and plunged into the ice. Bubbles were rising from the depths of the dark hole it had made in the glittering plain that covered the lake.

He walked over to what was left of the barrier and touched it, feeling the seconds wind back to before the crash through the chill of the cold metal, finding an appropriate moment to wind back to.

Anderson stood in the middle of the road watching the snowflakes melt on the black surface, he had less than three minutes before she would make the fatal turn and he couldn't think straight. All he wanted to do was get her to slow down, but he couldn't see her, the sleet was falling harder and swarmed around him as he strode forward along the road.

She was going faster than he anticipated. Her Ford appeared around the bend too quickly and he watched her eyes go wide as she saw him walking down the middle of the road.

The brakes were useless and her tires couldn't find any grip, she turned the car to avoid him and crashed through the barrier and into the lake.

. . .

'Now you know who caused the accident,' said a voice from behind him.

It was the colonel.

'I don't understand.'

'It's a paradox, I was sent to correct it. I'd hoped that your experience with the assassination would have taught you that the head-on approach never works.'

'I just wanted to slow her down.'

'So, go back and let her tires down before she leaves the house or steal the damn car. There are so many ways to influence the future without punching it in the face — you need to have a little finesse if you're going to join the Order.'

'You still want me to join?'

The colonel sighed. 'It's either that or have you screw-up even more history.'

'But —'

'Go back and hide her keys. I have work to do here.'

The colonel blew on his hands as he walked down to the shoreline.

'The farmer will be here shortly.'

He took off his coat. 'I think you'll find that was me.'

29

CONSEQUENCES

Anderson woke in his apartment to the sound of the shower running.

There were flowers in the vase on the dressing table and the sheets still smelled of her perfume.

The colonel had promised him things would be different, that he wouldn't always be able to tell what had changed. Anderson didn't care about the big things, all he wanted to do was lie there and listen to Isobel singing badly to the radio.

He had some hard choices to make about his future. They'd offered him a chance to join the Order and he was tempted, but it came at a price, he would have to leave this 'linear' world behind.

The consequences of their actions had led to a better life for him. Although he was still coming to terms with the devastation of the Second World War, he now had a sister who never died and a father who never drank himself into dementia.

The colonel said the memory of his previous life would fade, the longer he stayed in the present the harder it would be to remember the 'before', but there was nothing from that life he wanted to keep — apart from Isobel.

He explained that if Anderson refused their invitation to join the Order they would have to redact him. A seer would remove all the experiences of the past, their mission in 1776 — the knowledge that he could travel through time, all would be forgotten.

And that was the choice he had to make: to spend the rest of his days exploring the past, knowing that his parents, the Bureau and even Isobel would never know what he was doing or live a normal linear life.

Although all he could think about right now was how he'd just had the best night's sleep in years.

30

ROGERS

[King's Bench Prison, Southwark, London. Date: 1795]

Rufius Westinghouse walked into the courtyard of the King's Bench Prison, the paperwork for Rogers's release in his hand. The Order had limitless funds, and the old soldier's debt was nothing more than pocket change.

Colonel Rogers was a broken man. He'd returned to England with the last of the British troops and had spent most of the next decade in and out of Debtors' prison — there was no work in England for an old frontiersman.

Rufius could have come for him at any time. The tachyon that he stole from Anderson had the added benefit of being a tracking device. They knew every pawn shop and money lender that it had been hocked to over the last ten years.

But for some reason the ranger had always managed to get it back.

There were many destitute members of the aristocracy

walking about the yard. Their efforts to maintain a level of gentility in the degrading circumstances were pitiful. Their clothes were stained and torn, their wigs hiding shaved heads. The more recent inmates' eyes would light with hope as he passed them, praying for the benevolence of a stranger to lift them from their poverty, but there were many others who'd given up all chance of salvation.

The colonel tipped his hat to the warden as he entered the prison building. The man nodded and took the papers that were offered.

'Is he fit to travel?'

'He's not been fit for anything this past year.'

'Do you have any rum?'

The man looked a little surly. 'This is a Christian institution, sir. The partaking of alcohol is strictly forbidden.'

'It will make for a more passive prisoner,' Rufius suggested, handing him a half crown.

The officer considered the coin for a moment and then nodded. 'Follow me sir.'

Rogers was a sorry sight. Unable to stand without assistance, his clothes stained and soiled. He lay on the straw-stuffed mattress staring up at the ceiling.

'Colonel Rogers?' said the prison warden.

The man grunted. 'Now there's a name I haven't heard in a while.'

'A gentleman here with papers all signed. The debt is paid, you're free to go.'

'Is it now? And what would he be wanting from me in return?'

'I've come for the watch,' said Rufius.

'I thought that might be the case,' said Rogers pushing

himself into a sitting position. 'There was something about that device that bedeviled me. Like a lucky charm. I could never bear to part with it for good.'

'May I see it?'

The old colonel smiled and pulled it out on a chain. 'You've bought the right I guess. Though I'll trouble you for a shot of that rum in return.'

The colonel took the bottle from the warden and handed it to Rogers, taking the tachyon at the same time.

Rogers took a long drink from the bottle and sighed. 'So, you saved Washington this time,' he said with a wink.

31

PRESENTATION

[Battell Chapel, Yale University. Date: 2018]

Anderson's father stood on the stage. The cover of his latest book projected onto the screen behind him

'... no one knows what was discussed with the mysterious woman who demanded a private audience that night, but based on her information Washington had over forty loyalist conspirators arrested, including Hickey and two other lifeguards. Thomas Hickey was court-martialed on charges of mutiny and sedition. He was hanged on June 28, 1776, at the corner of Chrystie and Grand Streets before a crowd of twenty thousand spectators.'

His father took off his glasses, a signal that he was coming to the close.

'It would be wrong of me to speculate on what could have happened if they had succeeded on that fateful evening. There's no doubt that the repercussions of Washington's assassination would have been felt around the world.'

Anderson smiled, he knew exactly what could have

happened. He still had the memories of the other life, although they were fading, like a half-remembered dream.

They couldn't save Nathan Hale, but Samuel Fraunces had survived and later petitioned the Government for compensation as a reward for uncovering the plot to assassinate Washington. Governor Tryon and Mayor Matthews somehow escaped any involvement in the attempt.

It was only now, watching his father enthrall a lecture theatre full of academics, that Anderson realized that history was far from a set of concrete facts, but more a detective story pieced together from random documents by historians years after the fact. The further back you went the harder it became to be sure.

In a time before the internet and social media, when the revolutions weren't televised, the only records that seemed to survive were those that were written by the victors.

The colonel was right when he called it a wilderness.

There were so many parts of the past to be explored.

ALSO BY ANDREW HASTIE

The Colonel's adventures continue in Anachronist...

Josh has spent the last seventeen years trying to stay out of trouble and has failed miserably — one more strike, and he's going to prison. His mum is sick, and they're deep in debt to a local gang — there's nothing left to sell except for the TV, and that's the only thing keeping her sane.

Desperate, he breaks into the house of the local eccentric, the Colonel, and his life changes forever. Josh stumbles into the hidden world of the Oblivion Order, a secret organisation of time travelers sworn to protect the future by altering the past.

Moving back through time using ancient artefacts, Josh encounters extinction curators, memory vampires, houses with rooms in different centuries and Caitlin, a beautiful librarian who teaches him about the past and shows him a future he never dreamed he could have.

A fast-paced, time travel adventure, Anachronist will take you on a journey into a world not bound by the rules of time, exploring history and the consequences of changing it.

ABOUT THE AUTHOR

For more information about The Infinity Engines series and other Here Be Dragons books please visit: www.infinityengines.com

Please don't forget to leave a review!
Thank you!
Andy x

ACKNOWLEDGMENTS

Thank you to everyone who helped put this together. To Simon for giving me great feedback on this story and my wife, who continues to support me on this journey.

This is the first short story in a new series that I will continue to develop. In the meantime please check out my main series.